HOO HOO WHO?

written and illustrated by **Mary Maier**
also written by **Lauren Horton**

YOU'RE INVITED...

to Mouse's surprise party!

for Max & Murph

Hoo Hoo Who
Text copyright © 2018 by Mary Maier
Illustrations copyright © 2018 by Mary Maier
All rights reserved. Printed in Canada.

Building Block Press
Louisville, KY
www.buildingblockpress.com

Artwork is digital.
Text type is Verveine.

Library of Congress Control Number: 2018907435

ISBN: 978-1-944201-14-2

First Edition.

building
block

written and illustrated by **Mary Maier**
also written by **Lauren Horton**

HOO HOO Who?

Publisher's website and blog: www.buildingblockpress.com
Here you can find storytime plans for *Hoo Hoo Who?*, materials for teachers & parents, printouts for kids, and blog posts by both authors. This includes tips for encouraging expressive language skills by Speech Pathologist Lauren Horton.

Instagram: @buildingblockpress

SURPRISE!

oh. sorry.

My glasses are broken and I can't
see you too well.
I thought you were my friend Mouse,
but YOU'RE not Mouse, are you?

So – hoo hoo who are you?

Ahh! Hi, friend!

I'm so glad you could come.
Are you ready for Mouse's
surprise party?

Splish...Splash...Flap...Flap...

Did you hear that sound
outside the window?

Hoo hoo who
could it be?

Exactamundo!

It's Duck!!!

...with cake!? I just love cake!
Do you?

Hoo hoo!
Quack quack!

Hiss…Hiss…Slither…Slide…

What's that I hear now?

Hoo hoo who
could it be?

who has a scaly **diamond back?**

Who looks like the letter **S** ?

who says **hisssss**

...and is the **L O N G E S T** of our guests?

**DING!
DING!
DING!
Correct!**

It's Snake!!!

Snake certainly looks ready to celebrate! Party hats for everyone!

Hoo hoo!

Quack quack!

Hiss hiss!

Great Job!

It's Sheep!!!

...singing a happy birthday tune.

Hoo hoo!
Quack quack!
Hiss hiss!
Baa baa laaa!

That's NOT Mouse!

Hoo hoo who...or what... could that be?

A Package!!!

...for me?

for Owl

Now I can see all of you!

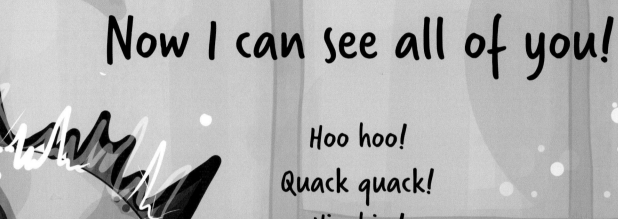

Hoo hoo!
Quack quack!
Hiss hiss!
Baa baa la la!
Squeak squeak!

Is everyone here?

Squeak squeak?

Let's sing
Happy Birthday
to Mouse!

Hoo
hoo!

What a day!
Thanks so much for
all your help!

Squeak squeak!

Hoo hoo who could ask for more wonderful friends?